LOVE AND WAR

(Arty's Story)

The Other Place Series, Book 3

By Elizabeth Roderick

LOVE AND WAR

Copyright © 2017 by Elizabeth Roderick.
All rights reserved.
First Print Edition: February 2017

Limitless Publishing, LLC
Kailua, HI 96734
www.limitlesspublishing.com

Formatting: Limitless Publishing

ISBN-13: 978-1-68058-995-5
ISBN-10: 1-68058-995-4

Dedication

For Mom and Dad.

If I waited to write a book that was appropriate to dedicate to my parents, we'd be waiting a long time.

I love you. Thank you for all you do for me.

Chapter 1

Dad sits there, Patient Zero of all idiots, with that smirk I always feel the urge to wipe off with sandpaper.

We're in some hotel bar in Albuquerque. It has terra cotta floor tiles, turquoise Kokopelli stencils around the ceiling, and a collection of dream catchers hanging from the peach-colored walls. It's a damn good thing they have tequila. I catch the waitress's eye and twiddle my empty shot glass.

Dad leans back in his chair, crossing his stubby legs. "So? What're you going to do now, Fireball?"

"You tell me, jackass. I thought that's why I was here, so you could boss me around."

The waitress brings my shot over, smiles as she sets it down. She's a little Mexican chick with a cute snub nose and nice, big tits. My dad scowls at me as I watch her walk away.

"How's the girlfriend holding up?" he asks.

"None of your fucking business." I throw back the shot. It burns my throat, settles warm into my stomach, and makes Dad almost bearable.

He shakes his head, grinning. "Sure, maybe not, maybe it's none of my business. You should have seen how that girl of yours came at me when she thought I'd killed you, though. If she weighed more than fifty pounds soaking wet, I'd almost have been scared."

I hold up my glass to signal the waitress again. "Look," I say as she jiggles over with another, "Liria's fine. I've got her hidden away out in California, handling a little branch of the operation. She's set up nice, has nothing to complain about."

Dad grunts and sips his scotch, and I take my shot. It sits sour. Liria hasn't got much to complain about, but she still does.

"You should take it easy on that stuff," Dad says.

I scowl. When your worst enemy is staring at you across a stupid polished-log table, it's not like you've got much to stay sober for. "Cut it, okay? I don't know why I'm here. I don't see what you want me to do. Just because that Polish sausage heard some rumor that I'm still alive doesn't mean he believes it. You talked to him, right?"

"Yeah, I talked to him. I calmed him down a bit. The problem was some border guard swore up and down he'd seen you."

I wince, and the booze burns my guts. "Raul, shit. I thought he looked at me funny. I should have given that asshole a bigger bribe."

Dad sips his scotch, shaking his head. "Jesus, Arty. You have to be careful. You just have no idea how to keep a low profile."

"I'm doing the best I can."

"Well you've got to do better than that. The last

thing we need is Czetski on high alert."

I massage my forehead with my fingertips. "The sooner we can get this shit over with, the better." I lay my palms on the table, lean toward Dad, and break into a slow grin. "And I might have that covered, anyhow."

Dad's eyes narrow. He gives me a little smile, leans back, and crosses his legs the other way. "Okay, Fireball, I'll bite."

Of course he will. "You know how whozits, Leonard Milliron, that old actor who had the huge comeback planned?" Dad watches me closely, twirling the ice cubes in his glass, and I continue. "He was gonna have a new series and a reality show and this and that. But then Zuhzuh-Czetski gets this opportunity with a hotter, younger actor, one whose infrastructure is a lot more amenable to money laundering. Guy's agent suggests a lineup of shows, but Zuhzuh couldn't do both this guy and Milliron's at the same time. The younger actor's agent is pushing for now or never. Add that to the fact that Milliron's attorneys think they've found more money for themselves in a couple of their contracts, and Zuhzuh decides to cut Milliron out of it."

A muscle in Dad's jaw twitches, and I feel encouraged. "Suddenly women start coming out of the woodwork, accusing poor Milliron of sexual assault. Horrible stuff about tying them up when they were drunk and watching while prostitutes put their mouths all over their naughties." The waitress gives me a quizzical look from over at the bar, and I nod and hold up my shot glass again.

"I should have hooked Milliron up with you,"

Dad says. "You would have been a willing participant."

"Fuck off."

The waitress comes over with my drink. "Having fun over here?" she asks.

"You know it, beautiful," I say, and she laughs and goes back to her post, where she seems to bringing cheer into the lives of a couple of dismal, balding travelers. She's looking better and better as the evening wears on, with hips and calves like she does Zumba or something.

"Anywho," I persist, looking back at Dad, who appears to have indigestion now, "Zuhzuh pulls out of all his contracts with Milliron and doesn't have to pay him a dime, because of the 'damaging behavior' clause. Whole thing is still tied up in court, of course, but Czetski got his contract with the hot young dude and is pulling in bank." I take my shot, and as it hits my belly and starts creeping up my spinal column, I know it has to be my last one. The world seems far away and vague, a cartoonish skit with a tinny laugh track.

"And it's too bad," I continue, trying not to slur. "It's bullshit, you know, because Milliron's actually a friend of mine, and I don't think he's tying chicks up and forcing them to get a cat bath from prostitutes. I feel like I sort of owe it to the guy to defend him, and make sure the real story gets out. Czetski's got a good network, but there are some channels that are still open and, you know, they'd open up further if we had some leverage. Racketeering charges are pretty damn serious, especially when they involve hurting the career of a beloved comedy icon. Nobody wants to be sitting on that ugly Polish ship when it sinks."

Dad just stares at me. He's the color of congealed beef fat, and it hits me that he's not young anymore. I wonder how long it'll be before we find him sprawled out stiff behind his desk, the telephone clutched in his hand, the voice of the poor sap that finally pissed him off all the way to hell still squawking over the receiver.

He settles back in his chair all relaxed-like, but he's not fooling me. "That's an interesting story. You find that one on the internet? Or, no, wait, it was obviously that girlfriend of yours, because she's a Czetski herself. Doesn't take a goddamn detective to put that shit together." He gives me a piercing look over the rim of his glass. "But you've apparently quit caring what happens to her, anyhow." He gulps down half his drink and puts it on the table. Condensation drips down its sides onto the grainy, blonde wood.

"Leave Liria out of it. It wasn't her," I say.

He rolls his eyes. "Yeah, yeah. But you go blathering that story around, she'll get hurt, and she's not the only one."

"I'm not going to go blathering it around."

"Looks to me like you already are."

My teeth clench. "What, to you? Going behind my back to Czetski wouldn't be good for your already failing health. Let's face it, Dad, you're too old to try to cut ties and live in hiding, and Mom would fly into a raging bitch about it."

"Why would I go behind your back? Jesus, Fireball. You're getting paranoid." He fixes me with his bullshit sneer.

I stare at him until he rolls his eyes and shifts in his chair. "Even if you're too stupid to realize it, you need me," I say. The world is spinning a bit, and I wish that waitress hadn't looked so nice bringing over shots.

"Yeah, yeah," he mutters. "What do you want to do then, Fireball?"

"Well, you called me out of fucking retirement saying I had to help you bring down Czetski, so let's bring him down. Together."

He chuckles. "That shit with Milliron isn't enough to bring Czetski down."

"If it were handled correctly, it would be. Zuhzuh's boss is probably looking for a reason to write him off anyway. Guy's getting old, and he's Polish, and no one likes that. Besides, it's not all I have: I'm not stupid enough to tell you everything."

Dad snorts and spins his empty glass. "Neither of us wants Czetski to go down just yet, Arty. We've got work to do before that happens."

"Speak for yourself. I've got my network in hand. I don't need him."

Dad's lips press together and his eyes glitter fiercely. "The fuck you don't need him. You don't know what you're talking about."

A wave of anger tries to lurch its way through the tequila, and makes it halfway there. "Don't tell me what I do and don't know, you fucking gnome." I press my fingertips into my eyelids for a moment before taking them away and again suffering the vision of my sneering father. "So, what?" I hiss between my teeth. "I'm just supposed to be doing your dirty work indefinitely, waiting for the supposed 'right moment' to finish the job with Czetski? I'm not your fucking mule anymore, Dad, and you don't get to fuck with me like this. Either we bring him down, or I'm out."

"All right, all right, calm down, Fireball." His gaze darts around the room, then fixes on me. "All I'm asking is you give this a couple months, okay? If we push him over the cliff now, it'll hardly be worth it for us. You'll have to retire in fucking Duluth instead of Barbados, and your mom and I will be a couple of putzes living on fixed incomes in Florida. You with me? We still have work to do."

I let out a long breath through my nose. "What work?"

"There's a couple connections we need to solidify, and we have to give the money time to get where it needs to go without him noticing."

My shoulders are starting to ache, and I roll my neck to work the kinks out. The thought of putting up with Dad for another minute makes retirement in Duluth seem like a viable option. But I sigh and try to find some patience. "I'll give you two months, and then I'm acting whether you're on board or not."

He shakes his head. "Good luck with that."

"Try me. Also, I'm going to visit Liria. I don't buy your bullshit about it being dangerous. I haven't seen any evidence Zuhzuh's having her watched."

"Your funeral. And hers, I should add."

"Take it or leave it, Dad. Otherwise, I'll talk to Milliron and his attorneys. It's all the same to me."

Dad stares at the table with a sour look, and my heart pounds, treading hard against the current of the booze. He passes his hand across his forehead and nods.

"Okay, Fireball. Two months. And go ahead, visit your poor girlfriend."

I have to stop myself from bouncing up and down in my chair. Instead I grin wide and watch Dad squirm.

Chapter 2

When I get back to the hotel room, Mary is sitting cross-legged on the bed in her underwear. Her wide, hazel eyes are fixed on the path of her scissors as she carefully cuts around a photo of a golden retriever in some tourist magazine.

"How did it go?" she asks vaguely.

"Pretty good." I sit next to her, and she wrinkles her nose because I've disturbed a pile of cuttings. She scoots away, gathering the pile closer to her bare thigh, and resumes cutting.

The tequila burns in me. Here I am, thirty-two years old, locked in a battle of wits with my fiendish father, and weighed down by a girl who doesn't notice I'm here unless I'm ignoring her. Liria is a thousand miles away and angry at me, and I'm adrift in this pastel-painted town.

I wander out through the sliding glass doors to the balcony. I pull out my phone and dial Liria, closing the slider so Mary can't hear, although I know she suspects I have someone. She doesn't seem to care.

The phone rings. The red, rocky hills around the city are tinged with the last light of the setting sun. The freeway hisses, evening commuters zipping across the bridge over the Rio Grande.

Liria answers on the fourth ring. "Hey, Arty." Maybe I'm just drunk, but she sounds different than usual. Happier, but a little breathless. A pang of suspicion hits me.

"Hey, sweet thing," I say, leaning on the iron railing. "How's it going?"

"Oh, you know." I let that hang over the airwaves for a moment, listening closely to her silence. The suspicion gnaws harder.

"I met with my dad today," I say.

"What? Really?"

"Yeah. And he and I have agreed you're probably not under surveillance. So I'm gonna come up there. You and I can work together now."

I expect her to squeal and jump up and down, but instead she snorts into the phone. "Arty, I don't want to do that. You said we were going to quit this stuff."

My stomach goes hollow, the booze snipping the long ends off my temper. "Liria, how many times…" I snort out a wordless curse. I want to throw the phone and watch it shatter in the parking lot below. "We've been over this a million fucking times, baby."

"Yeah, I know, and you have all your excuses. But count me out. I'm not fucking working that hustle anymore. I'll stay here, thanks."

My suspicion takes firm hold now. "Since when do you want to stay there? You've been bitching about it for months. And how is working there any different from running with me?"

There's a short silence, which feels like her grasping around in the dark for some way to save her story. "Arty…"

"What the fuck is going on, Liria?"

"Nothing's going on, I just don't want to run, all right? I don't want to be stuck here doing it either, but it's better than being out there on the road. It's a lot less dangerous here."

I breathe steadily through my nose. By the time I speak, I've worked most of the kinks from my voice. "Okay, Liria. That's fine. I understand. You don't have to come with me."

There's a pause. "Really?"

"Yeah, really. I've put you through enough already. Let's just forget about it."

"Thank you, Arty." She sounds relieved. "I love you."

We'll see about that. "I love you too."

I cut the call and lean there, watching the sunset's reflection off the lazy river. It's Dad's fault that things have gone sour between Liria and me. It's his fault we're back slaving away at this bullshit, instead of living in some white-walled Caribbean beach hut. I want to kick his balls all the way to the end zone.

***

The next day, Mary and I run up to Colorado Springs. She kicks back in the passenger seat with her big mirrored sunglasses on, singing along with

11

The Strokes. Her pink sundress drapes over her creamy thighs, and her pale arm sprawls on the windowsill. Her tattoos don't quite cover the track marks.

She pauses her singing. "Can we stop in Santa Fe? They have a really good artist supply store there."

"Fuck no, Mary. Jesus, the backseat's so full up with your fucking art crap I don't know how we're going to get at the shipment."

She purses her thick, red-painted lips and shoots me a lazy sideways glance over the top of the glasses. "Well, the cops won't fuck with us because we look like artists instead of drug runners."

Mary is really good at *looking* like an artist, all right. "Yeah, cops never fuck with sketched-out Bohemian freaks."

"Come on, Arty. It'll only take half an hour."

"I said *no.*" I'm a little sharper than I mean to be, and her lips twist into a pout. I sigh and pull my fingers through my hair. I hate the feeling of it since I dyed it black. Apparently I'm still recognizable anyway, so what the fuck. I should have kept the red.

"I'm sorry, Mary," I say. "I'm just run out. I'm gonna take a little break after this. I'll give you a little extra cash for a flight back to Milwaukee."

She tilts her head and fixes me with her deep hazel eyes. I think she's going to give me trouble, but she just shrugs and pushes the glasses up her nose. "Leave me in Manitou Springs. I know a guy there."

"You know a guy everywhere." She gets a tiny

smile on her face and I know she hopes she's making me jealous, but it's not going to happen.

We deal with the shipment, then I unload Mary with her friend: some guy in black skinny jeans and his hair cut to look like a cheap toupee. He hands me his card before I leave: "Scott Martin, ganjapreneur. Tours, sales, service." I toss the thing out the window as soon as I drive off, Mary's last, passive-aggressive kiss goodbye still burning on my lips.

I leave the car with a friend in Denver and catch a direct flight to San Francisco. I spend the first half of the trip fighting back images of Liria tangled up in the sheets with all four members of some punky girl band, their stupid silver lipstick smeared all over her body. I order a bourbon from the flight attendant and drink those thoughts from my mind. I don't think Liria would cheat. She's just not the type. But I am worried she's going out more than she should, making friends, letting herself get too well-known in the neighborhood. I also worry she may be cutting something off the top of the shipments I send her, squirreling away a little to sell on the side. Planning on running off when she's had enough of me.

I wince and order another bourbon. I've told that girl a million times that I'll get this worked out, that we'll ditch this game eventually, retire somewhere quiet together. But she's barely twenty years old, so patience and maturity aren't her strong suits.

I get a cab from the airport. The whiskey hasn't done anything to calm my nerves, and I'm just hoping against hope that Liria will jump into my arms and be happy I surprised her with a visit. But as I take the elevator up to the apartment, my adrenaline hums. I'm prepared for the worst. That she won't be there and won't come back for hours or days, or that she'll be on our bed, buried in a dogpile of Bay Area hipster girls.

I wipe my sweaty palms on my jeans as I get out of the elevator.

When I open the door to the apartment, I hear her voice, laughing. And another voice. A *man's* voice.

I find her in the kitchen with him. He's tall, young, with golden hair that curls all over the place. He's blinking at me with these blue eyes that have something weird going on with them. It sets off alarm bells whatever it is, only I don't really hear them right now, because I'm too frigging pissed off.

Liria's hair is dyed bright blue and, other than the fact she looks like she's about to piss her pants, she looks better than when I last saw her. Healthier somehow. Happier.

And that hurts.

"I knew it'd be some fucking bullshit like this," I say, but that's a lie. I had no notion she'd have a fucking *boyfriend*.

"Arty," she chokes out. The kid next to her is just staring at me like he's a two-year-old boy and I'm his pissed off mommy.

"Who the fuck is he?" I ask.

Liria raises her chin up and glares at me. "This is Justin." As if that explains it.

"What the fuck is he doing here?"

Her eyes glitter, and she gets a little maddening smile. "Staying with me."

Staying with her. I look back and forth between them. "Are you fucking nuts?"

"I've known him longer than I've known you, Arty. He helped me out once—"

"I don't care if he's your goddamn grandma. This is utter bullshit." The kid's probably just some pathetic goober she's taken in, but I don't know. He's too cute by half. And young. Her age. My teeth clench. "I should kill both of you."

"Oh, yeah, real fucking nice, Arty," Liria says. Her face crumples up and she starts to cry. "Go ahead, kill us. You're just like your fucking dad."

That sucker punch knocks my breath out. "Keep it down, or the fucking cops will come."

The kid has gone white. His eyes are unfocused, and his knees start to give. *What the hell?*

Liria steps over to catch him. "Look what you're doing to him!"

Maybe I learned that Darth Vader choking trick without knowing it, because the kid is collapsing all over the place.

"It's okay, Justin," Liria says, all care and concern. She puts her arms around him, sagging under his weight. I don't like the way she touches him.

"I should go," the kid says, and it's almost funny, because then he falls over. Liria loses her hold and he crumples onto his ass on the kitchen tiles.

"What the fuck is wrong with him?" I ask. He doesn't look drunk.

Liria sits next to him on the floor, holding him like he's some precious thing. "He's different."

"Different?"

"Yeah."

I dig my fingernails into the palms of my hands. "This apple-cheeked gimp your fucking boyfriend? Is that what this is?"

"*No,* Arty! And what the fuck would you care, anyway? You fucking leave me here, and I never see you, and you decide to show up *now*? You don't give a shit about me for the last three months, I'm just another of your hustlers, and suddenly you decide to kick on in in your jack boots and lay down the law?"

"What do you mean, I don't give a shit about you? I've been paying your bills, right? Calling you every fucking day. I don't do that with my hustlers."

"Not even every day," she says. "You call me a few times a week, maybe, and then it's just to fucking yell at me." She's crying hard, tears coating her flushed cheeks.

The kid's eyes roll back into his head and he slumps over. Liria tries to grab his shirt to keep him from falling, but he's too heavy and hits the floor with a thump.

"Justin!" She scooches over and puts her hand on his forehead, on his chest, feeling him all over. Either she's looking for the poison dart shot by some hidden pygmy or she just wants to touch him, I'm not sure.

"He's fucking different, all right," I say. "What kind of huge pussy of a man you got there, Liria? Faints if you just yell a little."

Liria looks up at me, and her eyes are like knives

in my heart. I've never seen her so angry. "You threatened to kill him, Arty! And you have a gun sticking out of your fucking pants! He thought you were going to shoot him."

I look down and remember my gun. I'm so used to it, I rarely think about it.

Liria leans back over this Justin boy again, tapping his cheeks with her palms, brushing his mess of curls back from his forehead. He's still breathing fine. There's nothing wrong with him, except that he's a wuss. I want Liria to forget about him, to look at me, instead, but not in that angry way. I want to reach out to her, to take her hand, but she's too busy fawning over this strange asswipe that's passed out on my kitchen floor. "Is he narcoleptic or what?" I ask.

"No. He's just…he has…I don't fucking know. This has never happened before. Justin, wake up," she moans. "Please. Please." She dithers over him with tears shining on her face.

My throat starts to close up, and I swallow hard. "Liria, who is this dude? If he really isn't your boyfriend, why is he here?"

"He needed a place to stay. His mom kicked him out, and he had nowhere to go, and he let me sleep at his house once when I was homeless. I couldn't turn him away." She's still looking at his slack face, not at me.

"You're risking everything just to keep some crazy jerk off the streets? Liria, that's bullshit—"

"No, I'll tell you what's bullshit, Arty." She finally looks at me. "You leaving me locked up here for months and months, telling me I can't even barely go outside, that I can't talk to anyone. Justin's cool, he's not a risk, and he..." She sniffs and wipes her eyes. "He's nice to me. He keeps me from going crazy." She starts crying harder. "I think we should call an ambulance."

I want to pull her off him and shake her until she rattles, but I take a deep breath instead. "He just fainted because he's a scared little bitch, that's all. I'm not calling the fucking ambulance, because the cops will come with them, and fuck that, Liria! Look what you fucking get us into."

Liria gasps as the kid twitches and opens his big blue eyes. He gets this little smile when he sees her there. It makes me feel hollow and sick, the way he looks at her, like I don't belong in the room, like I'm intruding.

"Liria, I'm okay," he mutters, and I'm thinking, *For fuck's sake, she's told this goober her real name.*

"Oh thank God, Justin," she breathes.

"Shitfucking Christ," I mutter.

He sits up, and Liria helps him. "Are you all right?" she asks.

"I'm fine, the Dark Energy just took me," the kid says.

Deep inside my skull, I finally hear the alarms clanging, and things start to clunk into place. The kid isn't different; he's fucking *mental*. She's taken in a goddamn *crazy* kid off the streets. I get dizzy for a second.

Liria looks a little confused too, and I wonder if she knew about him. "I didn't know the Dark Energy could do that," she says.

"Liria," I say, barely holding the puke down, "get him the fuck out of here. *Now.*"

Liria's eyes snap up to mine. "We'll both go."

The words hit me like a bullet, and my feelings bleed out. I remember all the times I've woken up with her beside me. All those lazy mornings we've spent cuddled up together doing nothing, just reading or watching TV and being together, and it was enough. It's never been like that with anyone else.

"Fine," I choke out. "Fucking fine. You'd rather be with this pudding-dicked retard than me? Great. Go. *Get out.*"

I want her to scream, to fight. I want her to refuse to go, to tell me she loves me, to tell me she hates me, anything, but just to stay, to keep talking. But she doesn't. She gets up, and helps the kid to his feet. "Come on, Justin. Let's get our stuff."

The kid's eyes fix on me as Liria tries to pull him out of the kitchen. They're the strangest eyes I've ever seen. He has this serene, sad look, no anger or violence in him at all, but I back off a step, my scalp prickling.

"Liria loves you," he says.

"Fuck off, Adonis," I snarl.

Liria tugs at his arm. She still won't look at me. "Justin—"

"Liria wants to stay with you, but this is too much hurt for her," he says.

I can't take it anymore. I turn and stomp into the living room, throw myself on the couch. There are cups and plates on the table, and I picture the two of them cuddled up together, watching cartoons,

19

laughing and eating pizza, like she and I used to do. I press the heels of my hands into my eyes.

They move around quietly, gathering their shit. I glance over at one point and see the kid carrying some blank canvases under his arm. So he's some sort of dickhole artist, then, like Mary. Maybe Liria will take a jewelry-making class and start wearing long drawstring crepe skirts. They'll live in a shitty studio apartment, paying rent out of his trust fund. Their friends will come over to drink chianti and talk in mystical tones about the muse visiting them in a dream and telling them to make collages out of broken mirrors and teacups.

My eyes fill up with tears.

I hear the front door open, and Liria's voice. "Bye, Arty."

The door closes, and they're gone. She's gone. I grab a plate from the coffee table and throw it hard against the wall. The sound of it shattering feels right somehow. I throw another, and another, *crash, crash*, the pieces tinkling all over the room.

Then I'm out of plates, and the apartment is quiet. Emptiness throbs through me, and I realize that sobs are tearing up through my belly. I fall on my stomach on the couch, shove my face into a pillow, and scream.

Chapter 3

I lie there for a long while until my head starts to clear.

I can't just huddle here like a chump. I'll be damned if those two are going to go pay rent on some fuck-nest with my money. I crunch over the broken china to my luggage and fetch my laptop.

When I get into Liria's bank account, she's already paid over three grand to a hotel down the street. She pulls out another two grand right as I'm trying to transfer the money out. I'm glad there's a limit on daily withdrawals, because that's the last she'll get out of this account.

Two grand won't get her far in this city, and she'll be back when she's broke. She never liked any job other than fucking people for rent and food, and the whackjob artist won't have shit for money.

After I put away the computer I don't want to think, so I tear through my medicine cabinets looking for something to knock me out. Liria's cleaned me out of Ativan, but I find a bottle of Seroquel with a few left in it. The bottle says the prescription is for Justin Flaherty. Maybe he'll end up in a straightjacket without them. Maybe then Liria will see him for what he really is.

I find a bottle of Knob Creek in my liquor cabinet, and swallow one of the pills down with a shot from the bottle. I wander around the apartment, taking more shots while I wait for the pill to kick in.

I find syringes in the bedroom wastebasket, and I kick it over, cursing, spreading dirty needles and wads of bloody cotton all over the floor. Liria had been hinting to me that she'd relapsed, or was going to. *Arty, I can't stand it. There's nothing to do but think, and I don't want to. I just want to knock my brains out of my head.* Well, I can't blame her, with the life she's had. But what did she want me to do? If Zuhzuh had been watching for her, leaving the house would have been dangerous. I was just trying to keep her safe.

I lie face down in my bed for a long time. The blankets still smell like her. I keep hoping I'll hear the door open, her voice calling to me: "Arty? I'm sorry…" But all I hear is the neighbors coming home from work, the cars driving by outside.

After a while, I get up, because it's hard to drink with my face in the pillow. The Seroquel is starting to pull its heavy veil over me, but I keep wandering the apartment looking for traces of her, of him, trying to piece together what their life together had been like. I don't want to know, but I have to. It's like a scab I can't stop picking at.

There's a lemon cream cake on the table in a pink bakery box, and half-eaten slices of it on the counter. That's probably what they were doing when I came. Eating fucking cake together.

She's left her blue t-shirt in the laundry basket, and a copy of *The Rum Diary* on the wing table beside the couch. There's a pencil drawing on the wing table too. It's of her, asleep on the sofa, sitting next to that friend of hers that got himself killed. Lee Harvey. Worst name ever. I stare at it a long time, wondering. It's really good. I mean, *really* good, or else I'm just high on these pills. I can see every grain of the wood floors, and the expression on Liria's sleeping face is just right. It's completely realistic, except for it has this tone. It's hard to describe; it's both bright and sinister.

I suddenly feel small and empty. I swerve into the spare bedroom, taking another swig of Knob Creek.

The bed is unmade, and find one dirty man's sock on the floor at the foot of it. Maybe it's just the Seroquel, but my guts settle down a little. Maybe she didn't lie. Maybe she and Justin were just friends.

But she still left with him. She chose him over me.

Some batshit, extremely talented artist, who looks like one of those little Greek playboys carved in marble, and with that gentle, lost look in his eyes like an abandoned kitten just begging to be loved and coddled and taken care of.

I fucking hate him. I want to crush his goddamn head. My fury is there. I can feel it stirring underneath the warm, fuzzy blanket of the pills and booze, and I almost throw the bottle of whiskey, just to hear that lovely shattering of glass. But I think better of it. I've made enough mess for one day, and I'll want the booze later.

I give it up for the night and collapse into my bed, her scent wafting up around me.

***

The next day, I wake up bleary and beat. I call the maid to come scour every last trace of Liria out of the apartment. I get rid of all the junkie trash first, though, because I've got enough problems.

I head out to meet with Fat Matt, one of the new guys I'm working with. He seems like a little bit of a moron, but I'm trying to cobble together a new network out of unknowns, so I can't expect to end up with a bunch of superheroes. It feels good to be out doing business, but as soon as I come home, the funk sets back in.

Yesenia has scrubbed her little heart out, and the place smells like Lemon Blast and bleach. The sheets are all washed, the windows cleaned, the coffee grounds chiseled from the kitchen grout. But I can still feel Liria and her artist boy here. Their life together has left imprints in the air, like a butt-dent in the sofa, and the place is empty, waiting for them to come back and laugh and draw pictures and eat cake.

My eyes sting. I head out again, slamming the door on that bad scene. I go sit in a bar and toss back shots of Glenlivit, wondering if I should try to pick up someone and take them home, just to push the ghosts out of the atmosphere there. But it would probably just make it more depressing, and besides, there's no one here but a couple of hipster dudes drinking PBR and a sullen fat woman sucking back a pint like she's had a shitty day at the office.

I could call Mary, have her come down and stay. Then maybe Liria would come back and find us the way I'd found her, laughing and eating cake in the kitchen. But Mary's a piece of work. I only hang out with her out of boredom and habit in the first place, and for help driving on the long stretches.

Besides, if I offered Mary a piece of cake, she'd suddenly decide she was gluten-free, or wasn't eating lemons because there's a strike going on in Bolivia or something. Then she'd wander off to browse the shelves of some secondhand store where the stuff's more expensive than new.

I slouch home with the whiskey hot in my belly, wondering how I'm going to get Liria back.

***

The next day, I go down to the hotel that Liria's staying at, the one that showed up as a charge on her debit card. The lady at the front desk was chosen to fit the clean-line modern décor, dressed in that sexy-severe way, short hair slicked back, her expressionless lips painted bright orange. She looks me up and down, takes notice of my five hundred dollar boots, and sits up a bit straighter.

"I'm here to see Christina Guzman and Justin Flaherty." I roll my eyes and smile sheepishly. "I forgot what room they're in, and I forgot my phone. I'm such an airhead sometimes…"

"I think I saw them leave a while ago, but I'll

call up to see." I watch her fingers closely as they dial, 1525, just in case I need the info later. She doesn't notice me looking; my shoes have made me trustworthy. Her green eyes hold my gaze as she hangs up. "They're not answering."

"Thanks for checking," I say. "I'm a little early, so I'll come back."

Her lips jerk into the semblance of a smile, and I wander back out onto the street. I find a place by the doors where the reception dominatrix won't see me loitering, and lean back against the warm bricks in the sunlight. Office workers and tourists and street kids go by. The streets are full of cars and bicycles, and the entire city steams with humidity. I almost like San Francisco better than New York.

I sink into thinking about business, mulling over the problem of how to solidify our network connections. I'm wondering about the guy named El Astrónomo down in Hermosillo, whether he'd be loyal to me, when Liria and the kid come around the corner.

She's talking and laughing, carrying another cake box. Jesus, they must really like cake. The artist is walking beside her, his big eyes on her. The way they look at each other makes me taste vomit. They're two kids, broke and living in a hotel, but they're not brooding and fucked up like I am. I'm just some bitter old woman Liria's forgotten about already, but they're happy just because they're together.

Liria sees me and stops, the smile draining from her face. The kid notices her reaction before he notices me, because he's only got eyes for her. They stand in the middle of the sidewalk, staring at me like I'm a monster that's popped out from under the bed.

"Cake again, huh?" My words grate through all the other things I want to say, which are caught in my throat. "Having a little party are we, on my dime?"

The blush on Liria's cheeks dries up, and her lips get tight. "Fuck you, Arty. You told me that money was mine, remember?"

"Yeah, well, that was before you cheated on me with this cheese dick."

Justin shifts from foot to foot, twisting a sheave of paperwork in his hands. I wince as I picture his long, sensitive artist's fingers all over Liria's body. "Our relationship isn't like that at all," he says, and he talks so quiet I can hardly hear him over the traffic.

"And what would you even care if it was?" Liria says. She stomps toward me, her brown eyes flashing. "You left me and ran off to goddamn Mexico or some shit for months—"

"I didn't fucking leave you," I say. "I had work to do, and it was safer for you here."

"Yeah, you had fucking work to do." She stomps, jouncing the cake box. "We could have lived forever on what we had, but you broke your promise. You said you'd give up that bullshit job, but you didn't."

The same fight, over and over and over. "You expected that money to last forever? Thought you could just lie around for the rest of your life, eating cake?"

"We could have if you hadn't let yourself get pulled back into that bullshit. If you hadn't fallen for your dad's fucking line of crap."

I close my eyes and take a deep breath. I want to tell her the whole story, but I can't. If she knows too much, my dad might have one of his little paranoid hissy fits and have her killed, especially if he finds out we're not together anymore and I don't have any control over her.

I open my eyes, my jaw aching from how stressful this all is. "If you'd ever worked a day in your life, you'd know how it was. I'm not going to explain it to you again." I push myself up off the wall. "Just stopped by to see how you two were getting along, if you'd spent all my money yet and were starving in the streets, but it seems you're not." The kid's gazing at me with his weird doe eyes, twisting and twisting the paperwork in his hands, and my anger fires up. "I really should have both of you killed. First whispers I hear that you haven't kept your mouths shut, and I will."

Lunatic Boy looks like he's going to faint again. Liria's giving me this look like she's trying to figure out whether I'd really kill her. At this point, even I don't know the answer to that question.

I can't stand the sight of them any longer, so I turn and walk back toward my apartment, where my bottle of whiskey is waiting.

Chapter 4

I take off the next day and go meet El Astrónomo in Puerto Peñasco. Without Mary to help with the driving, it takes me two days. I finally pull across the last dusty stretch of the Sonoran Desert and get down to the coast, the modest shacks giving way to the huge, luxury hotels piled up along the shore like pastel-colored flotsam.

I meet Astrónomo in a little seafood restaurant near the beach. I can feel eyes on me—the guy behind the bar, the woman waiting tables, a couple of older guys in the corner playing chess—as I walk to his table. Maybe they think El Astro is having an affair with some tourist, and they're wondering why he didn't pick someone younger.

He smiles as I sit down, then yells for the bartender to bring me a shot of their best tequila. "*Y la fuente de mariscos*," he says.

"*Sí, Señor*," the bartender says, tugging his white apron straight.

Astro nods in my direction, his eyes sparkling as he examines me. "I remember you like tequila. Do you like seafood?"

"Of course," I say.

He strokes his stubbly ghost of a beard. He's one of those flashy young guys who works balls-out, throwing his money around like a prince, expecting at any moment to end up dead or in prison. But he's lasted more than one good year—three now, in fact—because he's cautious. He doesn't pose on Twitter with his machine guns or kill people off the clock for stupid personal reasons. He might last a good long time, if he grows up just slightly.

And maybe he will if I give him a reason to, some vision of a future with me.

My tequila comes, but I don't touch it yet. "You know I'm not just here for the shipment."

"I had my suspicions that was the case."

I lean back in my chair. "How you like working for Lolo?"

He shrugs. His eyes are steady on me, astute. "It's fun. But I'm not, you know, married to the guy or anything. It pays a lot, but not a lot a lot." He raises his eyebrows, his smile teasing, waiting for me to lay it out.

So I do. I tell him about the upstart supplier and the small distribution network I'm building. "It's not huge, but there's not as many of us, so it pays better. You'd just have to keep your shit together, because I need reliable people, not playboys. I'm in this for the long haul."

He twirls his beer bottle in its puddle of condensation, frowning distantly. "It's dangerous," he says, his gaze darting up to mine, embarrassed to say it even though it's part of his ploy.

I nod. "But you can handle it. And I've got a friend in on this, high enough up that I'm not worried about having to pay too many bribes, or about a hit coming from anywhere but up top. If we're careful, we won't even get noticed at that level until we've hacked out our niche and cut Zuhzuh out of it."

"You want to cut *Zuhzuh* out of it?"

I nod, and he laughs.

"You're gonna have to tell me who this high-up friend of yours is, *Hadita*."

"You don't trust me?"

He quirks his lips. "Sure, I trust you, but you still gotta tell me."

I lean over the table. "It's *El Mimo*," I whisper.

His eyebrows shoot up, and he strokes his beard again. The waitress brings a huge, sizzling skillet of seafood and two plates, her veiled eyes looking me over as she sets it down. When she goes away, I purse my lips at Astro. "What, you don't believe me?"

"No, I think I do," he says. "I've always thought you had some sort of connection I wasn't seeing." He nods at the platter. "Try the scallops. They're really good."

I dish myself up some of the hot seafood, and he does also, his brow furrowing. He picks at his oysters thoughtfully while I eat a couple scallops. He's right; they're sweet and tender with spicy breading, and I've never had them better.

He sighs. "Okay, *Hadita*. I'll do it."

I can see by his nervousness that he's serious, and I grin and hold up my shot glass. "You'll be happy you did."

He toasts me with his beer bottle, and I take my shot.

I feel good. I feel one step closer to retirement. Closer to when I can tell Liria I'm really done with this shit, and that we're rich.

Astro offers to hook me up with a hotel room for a few days, but I'm feeling antsy. So after we eat I pull my car into the alley by the trashcans and load the duffels into the secret compartment, which is under the false bottom of the hatchback. Astro gives me a firm handshake and a flippant, white-toothed grin before I climb in. "We're going to make a good team," he says.

"Damn straight."

I leave him there with his hands in his pockets, watching me thoughtfully as I drive off. I hope he doesn't have a change of heart and double-cross me. But even if he were that type, I don't think he'd dare; not with my connections.

I start to get nervous as I get close to the border crossing. I'd asked Astro for the password, and it was different from the one they gave Dad, so they're on the lookout for me, or maybe just whoever else Dad is running across. I'm guessing it's me, though, which makes me even more nervous.

If I get caught and get *Mimo* in trouble with *El Enano*, then there's nothing that can save any of us. I'll just be another headless corpse in a pile somewhere along a Sonoran highway, Dad's pasty torso piled up next to mine.

And Liria. Jesus, I hope she's far enough out of

it, but she's a Czetski, for fuck's sake, even if she doesn't know what that means.

There's not much of a lineup at the crossing. I watch the cars ahead of me go through, my stereo turned down low, my foot tapping against the floorboards. I could try to run under the radar entirely, not give the password, just be another American tourist going back home. But I don't want to risk it. If word doesn't get back that I've crossed over, they'll get suspicious.

I pull up and smile at the guard, hand him my ID, a curled up wad of hundreds under it. I don't know this guy's name, but I've seen him before in my past life, and I send up a silent prayer that he doesn't recognize me.

I don't think he does, because a muscle in his jaw twitches in surprise when he feels the money there. He palms it as he gazes at my license, his gaze flicking to me. "Good afternoon, Miss Hanson. Going back home today?"

"Sure am. Can't wait to play a game of good old American golf." My spine tenses as I watch his reaction closely.

His eyes search mine, then he nods just slightly and hands me back my ID. "I love good old American golf too," he says. He breaks into a slow grin. "Have a safe trip."

And he waves me through.

I heave a sigh as I drive back out onto U.S. soil, pulling my fingers through my wiry-feeling hair and cursing my father for making me do this.

I turn up the stereo. Here I am, a thirty-two-year-old woman, streaking across the desert with thirty bricks of cocaine in the secret compartment of a Toyota. The bleak loneliness of it pulls my soul thin.

I've been running drugs for Dad for almost two decades now, and what do I have to show for it? My life is empty. It's a long string of hustles, punctuated by the occasional legal drama, business intrigue, and failed relationship.

I thought that would finally change when I met Liria. I could see myself having a life with her. Before, I hadn't wanted to keep running, but there had been no reason to stop. After all, it was money, and the work wasn't without its charms. Plus you can't just hand in your resignation for a job like this with two weeks' notice.

But Liria had been someone to quit for. She'd wanted to be with me, just the two of us together, a quiet life. And it had been good while it lasted too. I'd liked waking up every morning with the same beautiful, easy-natured girl beside me. I'd even started to think about one of us having a baby someday, buying a house in the country, with a garden and maybe a dog.

It had all fallen apart, though, and now here I am, back where I started. It feels like stepping back into dirty underwear after taking a shower.

And all because of that fucktard artist.

There's nothing for it but to pull off on a dirt road, park in the shade of a juniper tree, and dig into the stash.

A bump of coke reanimates me. It pours warmth into the cold emptiness. It tells me that, if I just get home, I can figure out a way to get Liria back.

I drive through the dwindling evening and into the night, pulling into the City just as the horizon is starting to glow. Traffic is easy and I slide into my quiet neighborhood, park in the garage under my building. My brain is bleary and disjointed, my thoughts running in circles. More coke won't help now. I just need to sleep it off, hope things look better in the morning.

A guy curled up in the corner rouses and tries to lurch to his feet as I wait for the elevator. I hadn't seen him there, and I get a jolt of shock. I think for a second I'm going to have to drop the duffels and reach for my gun. But the guy falls back down on his ass, his dirty legs sprawling on the stained concrete. He scowls at me like it's my fault. "I've got a doctor's appointment," he mutters angrily. "Do you know what it's like to have brain cancer? You don't know, you can't know."

My elevator comes and I climb in, the guy still yelling at me. I set down one of the duffels and wipe the sweat from my upper lip as the doors shut him out of my life. I wonder if Liria will be as into her crazy artist when he ends up like that guy.

My apartment door opens with a hollow sound. Everything is still, the smell of Lemon Blast still hanging faintly in the air. I shove the duffels in the hall closet, take a hot shower, and collapse into bed, my ears buzzing.

My thoughts are seething too much to fall asleep, and I have to get up and take another Seroquel to smooth them out. I fall asleep as the morning sun pours through the slats of the shutters.

***

The afternoon is getting ripe by the time I wake up. I haul myself out of bed, take another shower, and call Schnoz. Then I fill myself full of coffee, sitting alone in my kitchen, thumbing through *The Rum Diary.*

There's a knock at the door as I'm finishing my third cup, and I get up to answer it. Schnoz is standing there with his hands in the pockets of his cargo shorts, grinning. "Hey, '*dita.*"

I let him in, offer him a cup of coffee. He puts in a gallon of cream and shovelful of sugar, then sits hunched over my kitchen table. "Wasn't expecting to hear from you," he says as he slurps it down. "What happened to the brown-eyed girl?"

I shrug my stiff shoulders. "She's out and about. You might see her again."

"Wouldn't mind that." He grins and I have to resist the urge to smash his mug into his teeth.

After he leaves, I pack a couple grams from the quarter I held back and head down to see my friend Stewart. When I get to his art gallery, I find it all torn up, plastic all over the floors, his employees slathering paint on the walls with rollers while he stands there berating them. "How do you ever expect to get your MFA if you can't even paint a wall? Look at this, it's got more drips than an insurance agent convention." He looks over his shoulder as I walk in. "Arty!"

"Hey, Stewart."

"Oh, honey, I missed you." He comes over to squeeze me in his wiry arms. "How have the travels been?"

"Fine, fine."

He holds me at arm's length, searching my face, his lips pulled back in an uncertain smirk. "Let's go into my office."

We head through a door in the back, Stewart yelling at his employees that he wants them to be finished with the paint job by the time he comes back out.

"What are you doing in here, anyway?" I ask when we gain the quiet of his office. "Looks like you're remodeling."

His hands fidget with the lapels of his sport coat as he sits down behind his desk, and I get an unsettled feeling. I plop into a chair and raise my eyebrows.

"I have the opening of an exciting new artist coming up," he says, and his eyes dart to the corners of the room. "I actually thought you knew already."

A sick feeling blooms in my stomach. "What's up, Stewart?"

He sighs and pinches the bridge of his nose. "I'm really sorry that you and Christina had…you know, a falling out. But now I'm bound by a contract…and besides, he's an *excellent* artist…"

"Your new artist is this Justin kid that she's with now?" I say hoarsely. So much for her crawling back when they run out of money.

He squirms. "Wait, what? They're not actually, you know, *together*, are they? I mean Christina likes cock slightly less than I like pussy."

I chew on my lip, wondering if this is an act. "A woman can change her mind. She's had boyfriends

37

before."

He waves this idea away, a smile twitching his lips. "You're just being paranoid. She told me they were just friends."

I sit considering this. "Huh," I say, and he winces.

"Come on, Arty, don't be mad."

"I'm not mad."

He watches me with a veiled look. "I had no idea it would turn out all drama like this. When I signed him up, I didn't even know he and Christina knew each other."

I clench and unclench my fists. "How did that go down, then?"

"He's the boyfriend of a friend of mine's niece," he says, and my nausea eases somewhat. "I saw some pictures of his paintings, and I knew I had to have him. But when he came in, he showed me this drawing of this girl that looked just like Christina. Said she was someone he'd met a while back, but he didn't know her name. So I…I called Christina in to see if it was the same girl, and it was." He rubs his nose, avoiding my gaze. "He needed a place to stay or he'd be homeless, so Christina said she'd take him in."

I cross my legs, fold my hands on my knees. "Sounds pretty innocent."

"Arty…" He gives me a pained look, and I smile.

"Don't worry about it, Stewart. I don't expect you to take sides in my fucked-up love life. In fact…" I tug the baggies of coke out of my jeans pocket, toss them across his desk. "I love you so much I brought you a present."

He breaks into a wide grin and claps. "You shouldn't have!" The grin fades. "Wait, is this, like, for free?"

"As a bird. Although I do have a proposal for you."

His hand hesitates over the baggies, watching me closely. "A proposal?"

"Remember way back when you said you wanted to unload some product for me, but I said no because you're such a turd? Well, I've changed my mind."

His mouth forms a little "o". "Are you serious?" He giggles breathily. "But, wait, why?"

"Just between you and me, I'm setting up a new network, so I need new people. When I saw you doing all these renovations, I thought to myself, it can't be cheap, that maybe you'd like the opportunity to make a few extra bucks. You've done a good job for me, running money through this place, and deserve a bigger cut."

He fiddles with the baggies, rubbing them between his fingers. "Okay. So, what, then? How much do you want me to sell? And do you need the money up front or…"

"I've got a quarter brick for you. And don't worry about money up front. Pay me seven when it's sold."

I can see him doing the math in his head. He nods. "Okay."

I grin and hold out my hand, which he shakes, although he looks a little pale, the sweat starting to bead on his forehead. "It's going to be great doing business with you," I say.

He smiles uncertainly. "I hope it doesn't ruin our friendship."

I snort. "We've been partners this long, and it hasn't."

"Yeah, I guess that's true." His shoulders relax slightly.

"I'd like to see this Justin guy's artwork, though."

He blinks. "You would?" Then he breaks into a grin, his enthusiasm pouring out all over his face. "Of course you would. However you feel about him personally, the man's a genius."

He jumps up and I follow him into the storeroom.

He has a stack of framed drawings, and he starts showing them to me, but it's one of the oil paintings leaning against the walls that draws me in. It's of Liria curled on the couch, surrounded by a mass of terrifying images that seem to be in the process of solidifying out of the air.

Somehow I know what the painting is about, because I've been there. It's about her being dopesick, about her kicking heroin. Things start to fall into place. She isn't getting high any longer, which is why she looks so healthy. "How much for this one, Stewart?"

His smile freezes. "It's not for sale yet. You'll have to come to his opening, which is coming up."

"No deal. This one's mine." My eyes lock on his. "How much?"

He rubs his chin. "There's a lot of interest in his work. I wouldn't let this go for less than ten grand."

I give him a tight smile. "Make it seven. The

coke's yours free and clear, just give me the painting."

His lips tighten. "I have a contract with him, Arty. I can't undersell him, it'd be dishonest."

"Yeah, but you're paying him, what, fifty percent of sales?"

"Sixty," he mutters.

I raise my eyebrows. "Still, you're making out. Listen, I'll make it eight and a half. I'm letting you have the coke under market, anyway. I'll give you fifteen hundred and the coke, and you give me the painting."

He still hesitates, and it strikes me that maybe he wasn't bullshitting me on the price. Jesus fuck, ten grand for a little oil painting from an unknown artist. The kid's good, but I had no idea there was that sort of money in him. Finally, Stewart nods, though he doesn't look happy. "I'll do that, because we're friends and business partners. But you can't take it until after the opening."

I nod. "Deal. And thank you, Stewart."

His brow is furrowed, but then he breaks into a sort of teasing smile. "And if you're so stuck on Christina that you need a painting of her this bad, why don't you work it out with her? It's not like you're an art collector."

I sigh, rubbing my hand over my face, and he laughs sympathetically.

"Oh, Arty, you're in love," he says. "It's finally happened. Stop fucking it up, whatever you're doing, and get her back."

"Yeah," I mutter. "Yeah, I'm working on it." I make myself grin. "Can I see the rest of this kid's drawings?"

"As long as you don't clear me out of them. Leave me something to make money on."

I laugh. "Of course, Stewart."

He shoots me an uncertain look as he lays the drawings out for me to see. I peruse them, a plan solidifying in my mind.

Chapter 5

Stewart unloads the product very efficiently, which doesn't surprise me. His crowd are the only ones who haven't switched to meth or Adderall yet.

Stewart's got good business sense, up to a certain point. But he's in over his head this time, because my business sense is quite a few points higher than his.

Meanwhile, Astro makes his first run down to my new supplier, and brings me back a shipment. I meet him at a house in Fresno, where he greets me with a big grin and a hug. "*Hadita*, my favorite girl."

I laugh. "I like to hear that."

We load the stuff into my Toyota, and he's practically gushing cheerfulness. "I like the new guy, and his stuff is excellent and fucking cheap. I feel good about my prospects in this venture."

I close the compartment and smile at him, slipping him a wad of bills that's even bigger than he was expecting. "I don't disappoint."

When I get back into the City, I amble into

Stewart's gallery and find him having a conniption.

"Not there, you pathetic moron!" he screams. One of his employees, a skinny girl who looks about twelve, can barely stay on her ladder for all her trembling.

"But, Stewart—"

"Never mind, Ghana, just patch the damn hole and paint over it again." He sees me and smiles. "Oh, hi, Arty."

"Hey there, cupcake," I say. "Not interrupting anything, am I?"

Stewart rolls his eyes and runs his fingers through his short, brown hair. "Just a circus act of brain-damaged clowns. Come on, let's go into my office."

We head into the back, leaving his employees to likely conspire against him in a huddle. He sighs heavily as we plop down in office chairs.

"Right on track for the opening, it seems?" I ask.

He grimaces. "This thing is going to be big. Huge. I want to make sure it's right."

I keep my face blank. "It can't be that big. Kid's an unknown, right? You discovered him."

"And I'll go down in history books for it. You should have seen the write-up he got in *The Chronicle*. Paul Legrange was creaming his panties about him, and now I've got a guy coming in from *The New York Times*. Plus, there's all sorts of dealers and agents and other vultures circling. Just yesterday I had someone offer me thirty grand for my contract with him." He runs his hand over his face. "Normally, I'd jump at something like that, but in Justin's case, I don't think so. The boy churns out like ten pieces a month, and I'm liable to make way more money than that. Besides." He smiles. "You probably don't want to hear this, but the boy's a sweetheart, without an ounce of ego. He has no idea what he's worth, and doesn't care. If I ask him for another exclusive contract at the end of the six months, he's going to do it."

My heart's beating a little faster, but I keep my expression as one of polite interest. "It's not very nice to take advantage of retarded boys, Stewart."

He snorts. "Oh, Arty. Don't let this misplaced jealousy sour your naturally sweet nature. He's a little...off...but he's really smart. He's got the business sense of a newborn puppy, though. I'm doing him a favor, taking care of his affairs."

I study him a moment. "A little bit off is right, Stewart. When I walked in and found him living in my apartment, you can imagine I was a little bit surprised. Maybe I yelled a bit, you know, but it was enough to send the kid into a spiral, and he collapsed and woke up saying some really weird tinfoil hat shit." I twist the end of my braid in my fingers. "He might be more of a liability than you think, at least long-term."

He laughs. "You may know drug-running, Arty, but you know *nothing* about my business. Justin could collapse in a heap at his opening and start screaming about the second coming of alien Jesus, and he'd still be less drama than most artists. It might even add to his mystique."

I nod. "Touché. However, speaking of drug-running..."

He pushes his glasses up his nose. "Thanks for

that deal, by the way. Easiest money I've ever made."

"You think you could handle a whole kilo?"

He glances around like he's paranoid there's a federal agent crouching behind his Crate and Barrel bookcase. "What, you have more already?" He licks his lips. "I mean, sure, I'm busy, but I could handle it. Hell, give me two kilos if you've got them."

I smile. "I do. I'll bring two bricks over, then. Give me fifty-four grand when you've got it sold. Sound good?"

His eyes shine at the thought of all that money, though I can see the sweat popping out on his pale forehead. He may be nervous, but he doesn't know the half of it.

"Sounds excellent, Arty," he says.

"I'll bring it over this afternoon," I say.

***

That night I call a girl named Loretta who I met through Stewart a few years ago. She's one of those artists who paints crucified squirrels, her long-suffering parents paying for her MFA, which is taking her five years to achieve.

She answers sounding groggy, like I woke her up at four in the damn afternoon. "Arteeee! You're back! I've missed you. Come meet me for a drink."

So I meet her at one of those pseudo dive-bars. San Francisco hipsters say it's working class because they have taxidermy on the walls and shots for less than fifteen bucks. Loretta is hunched over a plate of tater tots at the bar, sucking down a beer and watching soccer on TV, but she bounds off her stool when she sees me.

"Oooh, love the hair, you look awesome." The buttons and badges on her denim vest poke my belly as she grabs me in a rough hug. "Come on, sit down, I'll buy you a drink."

"Let's get a booth, pop tart. I don't want the bartender to overhear us talking dirty."

She grins, showing cute, crooked teeth. "Oh, Arty, you slut."

She grabs her beer and food and we slide into the vinyl bench seats. The bartender struts over, mussing his hair and showing off his tattoos, and I order a shot of Crown with a back of Diet Coke.

Loretta nudges me with her bright red sneaker. "So? What you up to?"

I shrug. "I'm in town for a while. Work took me down to South America, but I have a few weeks or months off, so we'll see."

She chews a tater tot, her eyes wide. "I'm so jealous of your job. The personal assistant gig sounds fucking solid." She wrinkles her nose and pouts. "Why won't you tell me who you work for?"

"I signed a nondisclosure clause, you know that. I'm not going to risk this job telling a loudmouth like you."

She bounces in her seat. "Oh, come on. Is it Robert Downey Jr.? It's Robert Downey Jr., right? Oh, my God, that would be awesome."

I just smile mysteriously as my whiskey comes, and she rolls her eyes. "Fine, be that way. You're probably not telling me because it's someone lame."

I snort and I take my shot, and I know I've been

drinking too much lately because I hardly feel it. "So, uh, hey," I say, putting down my glass. "You wanna get some coke?"

Her eyebrows shoot up, and she leans over the table. "Hells yes," she says in a stage whisper.

"You know where to get some? My connection seems to have dried up."

She pulls out her phone, smirking at it as she types out a text. "Stewart's dealing now."

I quirk my lips. "*Stewart's* dealing now? You're fucking joking. What, is his gallery going under? Or has he just gone off the deep end?"

She gives me a bright-eyed look. "No, his studio is doing really well. He has this amazing new artist he's doing an opening for. You should see his stuff, it's like…" She pauses, her eyes glazing over. "I don't even know. It's like he's painting this fantasy world, except it's more real than reality, and it tears at your guts, the way he does it. I can't describe it. He's a genius." She shrugs and goes back to her text. "I don't know why Stewart's dealing when he has that going on, but I don't try to figure that crazy fucker out."

It's all I can do to keep the shit-eating grin off my face. "Don't tell Stewart I'm here," I say. "I don't want him to know I'm doing coke. He always yells at me."

She raises her eyebrows. "That's sorta pot/kettle, right?"

I rub my nose sheepishly. "Yeah, well…I used to have a problem, you know. He's just being motherly."

Loretta shrugs, sending the text. "We've all got

problems."

***

We catch an Uber, and when she gives the driver the address, I settle back in my seat, chewing my lip. He's dealing it out of his boyfriend's condo. I should have suspected, especially since he mentioned that Jack's in New Zealand right now. Stewart spends most of his time there, anyway. His house is way over in Marin, and he only keeps it for someplace to escape to on off days.

I stretch out in the back seat of the car while she goes up to meet him, and sit chatting with the driver about the best places to live in San Francisco. He laughs about not being able to afford even the worst places.

It doesn't take Loretta long, and soon I'm pulling my legs off the seat so she can jump back into the car. "Got my phone," she says. "All set."

We'd told the driver she'd left her phone at our friend's house and were just going back for it, but he squints at us, and I know we're not fooling anyone.

We go to Loretta's place, put on some Django Django, and proceed to get pretty damn high. Loretta's fun and cute, and a pretty good fuck, but she's too into toys for my taste, and she's not Liria.

I head back home at dawn, strung out and bleak-feeling. I want to pop another of those pills and turn my brain off for a few hours, but I can't yet. First, I get a hold of Gunnar, who's this shit-for-brains junkie, as fucked up and scuzzed out as you can get and still be reliable. And I don't mean reliable like you'd ask him to babysit your toddler or even take care of your houseplants for the weekend, but the guy does get shit done. In fact, getting shit done is a sort of twisted, criminal superpower he has, and half the time I'm not sure how he manages to do what he does and stay alive and out of jail.

You've got to watch him, though, or he'll rip you off as part of the deal. He'd try to lift your wallet even if you had a gun to his head, telling him not to. He just doesn't care. Guy would jump off a fucking cliff into a pile of shit and broken glass for half a gram. I have qualms about trusting him on this, but for what I have in mind it'd be too risky to go further up the criminal ladder.

I meet him at a coffee shop that I never go to, ten blocks away, because no fucking way do I want this guy to even know what neighborhood I live in. He shuffles in with the cuffs of his jeans dragging around his ankles, running his hands through his startlingly fucked-up hair. Gunnar takes bedhead to a whole new level: not mussed by a gentle fuck between clean sheets, but by a brutal gang rape in a dumpster behind a bad Chinese restaurant.

He grins at me, his grey teeth showing, one of the front molars missing. "Hey, Annie," he mumbles sleepily. "You look beautiful, girl. Love the hair."

I buy him a coffee and a donut, try to assume an expression that might suggest to onlookers that I'm giving charity to a homeless guy in some fit of WASP-y guilt.

He sprawls out indecently in his chair, snarfing

his donut. "So, what's up, sweet thing? Where you been, huh?" He wipes his mouth on the back of his hand, but it just smears the crumbs around. It physically hurts to look at him but I manage it, even force a smile.

"Oh, you know," I say, shrugging. Then I let the smile die a natural death. "Listen, Gunnar, I got a job for you."

He leans over the table, a dull, animal greed lighting up his eyes. "Well, all right."

So I lay it out for him, using what I hope is just the right balance of death threats and promise of reward to maximize my take on the deal. Then I scrape the bastard off and head back to my apartment, pop a Seroquel, and sleep until late afternoon.

I hear from Gunnar that evening. "Hey, tootsie roll, I got a present for you."

I let out a breath and smile to myself. He doesn't waste time. "Aw, you shouldn't have."

I meet him in a grocery store parking lot, and we load the bag into my Toyota. I open it, and I see there's about a quarter brick less than I was expecting. I raise an eyebrow at Gunnar, who's shuffling his feet, his rheumy eyes following the progress of a pigeon across the darkening sky. "What the fuck is this, Gunnar? You ripped me off more than half a kilo."

His pinpoint gaze slides across mine. He purses his lips in a halfhearted attempt to look affronted. "That's what there was, Annie! What the fuck, you can't ask me to steal what's not there." I raise my eyebrows and he glares at me, his eyeballs twitching. "Fuck," he spits, stomping his dirty sneakers on the pavement. "This is bullshit, Annie—"

My gun is out and pressed against his flaccid gut before the he can even stop whining. He stumbles, his hazy, brown eyes wide. I don't like being this close to him because of the smell, so I hope it doesn't take long to get through to him. "Now listen, you fucker, it's damn nice of me to give you these jobs, and to hold up my end of the deal with payment. It'd be easier to kill you than to pay you, because who would notice, Gunnar? Who would care?"

"I've got more people than you can imagine—"

"Cut it, asslicker. I'm gonna give you half of the three grand we talked about, and consider yourself fucking lucky. You ever think about ripping me off again, ask yourself first, do you think they've got good dope in hell? Because I'm guessing all they've got is chicken shit mixed with Folgers Crystals, and you can slam it until you piss brown without catching a nod."

Sweat drips off his forehead, and he's starting to smell even worse. "Fuck, Annie—"

"Fifteen hundred or death, Gunnar. Choose."

His lips tremble, but he nods. "Okay, whatever. Jesus."

I pay the guy, and then I get in the car and drive off, cursing. I have to do that shit with Gunnar every. Fucking. Time. I'm just glad he's not smart or ballsy enough to pull off a good screwjob, because then I'd have to go find myself another lowlife idiot savant.

I hide the coke under the floorboards of my closet, along with the other five kilos I haven't unloaded yet. I think I'm going to fling the shit at this chick I know up in Seattle, but I haven't had time to set it up. This whole deal with Liria has gotten me distracted. My dad would have my ass if he knew.

It's the middle of the next day before Stewart has the balls to call me. He's practically in tears. "Arty, you'll never believe what happened...I swear I'm not lying..."

I keep my voice tense. "What's up, Stewart?"

He heaves a horrible sigh. "Can you just come down to the gallery? I'll talk to you here."

When I get down there I find him huddled in his office, pale and sweaty, a man in ruins. I want to offer the poor guy a drink or a cigarette, but instead I sit down across from him, cross my arms, and raise my eyebrows.

"Arty—"

"This is obviously about my money, so just tell me, Stewart. I didn't bring my gun, so you're not going to die today; I've got an appointment later and wouldn't be able to make it back here on time."

He collapses with his head in his hands and then looks up at me, his lips tight. "I got ripped off last night. The coke's gone."

I suck air between my teeth. *What?* Oh, my fucking *God*. Stewart, how could you let that happen?"

He wrings his hands, writhing in his seat. "I can't help it. Someone broke in. I had the alarm system set—"

"*Alarm system*? Alarm systems aren't worth shit. A three-year-old could disable them. Did you have it in the same place you were dealing from? Did you just have it in a closet or something?" His face crumples, and I squeeze my eyes shut, my hands gathering to fists on his desk. "Two bricks of coke in a fucking closet, where every lowlife tweaker knows to look for it? For fuck's sake, Stewart…"

"Arty, I'm so sorry." He actually has tears in his eyes. I feel sorry for him. He's an upper-middle-class art gallery owner, getting his first taste of the real world, and I'm sure it sucks.

I put my hands over my face for a long moment before giving him a level look. "I should have known you weren't up to this. I thought you had more sense than a retarded rock, but I guess I was wrong."

He doesn't say anything, just sits there staring at his lap and shaking.

I sigh. "You know what? I want to make this right. You've been my friend for a long time. I want to find some way to not be in a murderous rage about this."

"I'll do anything," he says quickly. "I don't have fifty-four grand right now, but I'll pay you in installments…"

"I'm not Chase Manhattan, Stewart. This isn't a fucking home loan. Installments don't work, because if I don't have the cash for the next shipment, I'm toast. You've put me in a fuck-all position."

He winces and looks back at his lap. I let him stew in it for a while before I speak again.

"But, you know what? I'm tired of this business anyway. This might be a good chance for me to branch out, get involved in something new."

His eyes crawl up to meet mine, a pathetic spark of hope kindling in them. "What do you want, Arty?"

So I tell him.

Chapter 6

The day of Justin's opening, I walk in to find the place packed like a fucking disco, except it's a bunch of people with carefully crazy hairdos, clothes of fair-trade organic cotton and hand-woven sustainable bamboo fiber. I gaze around, but don't see Justin or Liria anywhere.

Stewart, who is deep in conversation with an old lady in some sort of silky, flowered wizard robe thing, makes his excuses to her and rushes over to me. A look passes between us. "Arty, there you are."

"Good turnout," I say.

He rubs his nose sadly and nods. "Yes. Justin's going to be very big. He's a genius."

I squeeze his shoulder. "Cheer up, Stewart, you'll get your cut, even if it's smaller than you want."

He winces. "It's not even that."

I pat his back. Stewart truly is a good guy. He tries hard and he really cares about this art shit. "You'll go down in the history books as the one who found him, don't worry."

He grins at me and rolls his eyes, but I can see from his expression that's all he cared about to begin with. Jesus. With priorities like that, no wonder he's easy to rip off.

"Speaking of the boy genius, where is he?" I ask.

Stewart's brow gathers up into furrows as he scans the crowd. "I don't know. I have no idea. That's weird."

I open my mouth to say I'm going to go look for him when Stewart's face freezes, his gaze fixed at a point over my shoulder. I get a prickle on the back of my neck.

I turn, and it takes me a second to regain my composure. Two sheriffs have just walked through the door. I don't know either of them—it's a woman with a brown ponytail and a thin squiggle of a mouth like Charlie Brown, and some ham hock of a middle-aged dude, his belt an equator line around his ridiculous waist. They stand looking around the room, the woman holding a sheaf of papers. The polite chatter of the crowd quiets a bit as they notice them, sending them curious glances.

Stewart whisks over to the cops in a hurry, and I follow behind.

"Hello, I'm Stewart Califax, the owner of this establishment. May I help you?"

The woman cop's eyes flick to me. "We're here looking for Justin Flaherty. We have information that he'd be here tonight."

I chew my lip. The kid didn't flip out and murder someone did he? That would be expensive on my part, because I'd lose most of my investment, but at least it would get him out of the way.

Stewart opens his mouth, closes it, then clears his throat. "Well, yes, I believe he is. May I ask why you're looking for him?"

They fix him with their lizard cop stares. "It's a legal matter concerning Mr. Flaherty, and we'd like to discuss it personally with him," the woman says.

The crowd is still trying to look disinterested, but their stares are even more curious. This could be bad for publicity. "Stewart and I are his managers," I say, giving the cops' bitchy power-trip stare right back. "If you want access to him, you need to tell us the reason." I take a gamble that the little twerp didn't have the balls to do anything violent. "Somehow I doubt that you're here to arrest him on a criminal matter, so it's inappropriate for you to be here disturbing his business dealings in the first place."

"I'm sure we can resolve this amicably, whatever it is," Stewart says, hands fluttering. "But you're either going to need to tell us your business, or show us a warrant."

The cops exchange a tired glance. "I have a guardianship petition to serve on Mr. Flaherty, filed by his mother," the woman says. "We're also here to take him into custody on a psych hold."

Stewart and I look at each other. "I'll go find him," he mutters. "I think he must be in the back."

I nod. "I'll come with you."

The cops follow us through the crowd toward the office door. Stewart smiles around at everyone. "They're here to arrest us all," he says, laughing, and I have to admire how he manages to seem truly unconcerned. "I'm just joking, you guys, it's nothing to worry about. We just had a problem with the alarm earlier."

It's quieter by the back door, and he turns to the cops. "Wait here a minute, I'll see if he's back there."

"I think we'll come with you and check," the guy cop says.

"You don't have permission to do that," I say. "The back of the building isn't a public space, and you need a warrant unless you're invited." Stewart and I exchange a significant look. I figure he wants to have a word with Special Boy before springing the cops on him so he doesn't faint or start speaking in tongues.

The man cop glares at me. "I'd appreciate it if you wouldn't tell us what the law is, Miss…"

"There's no back door. I'm not going to help him escape," Stewart cuts in.

The woman cop's lips twitch, but she and her partner exchange a small nod. She shrugs. "All right."

I cross my arms and gaze silently at the crowd. The cops don't try to make conversation, but just stand there thinking their jerkoff idiot cop thoughts, whatever they are. After a few minutes, Stewart returns. "He's in there. You can come in."

We file into Stewart's office. Liria is there with pretty boy. Holding his fucking hand, even, their fingers intertwined like lovers. It's like being punched in the guts, but I keep my face still. I smile.

"Justin Flaherty?" the female cop says.

"Yes, that's me," the kid says in a voice so quiet

you can hardly hear him. He's clutching Liria's hand, his blue eyes shining with childlike fear.

The chick cop hands him the paperwork. "We're here to serve you with a petition for guardianship. Your mother, Jane Flaherty, has filed a petition with the San Francisco County Superior Court to be named as your legal guardian and the manager of your personal finances, alleging that you lack the capacity to do so yourself."

Liria huffs, and the kid takes the paperwork, stares at it blankly.

"Your mother has also filed a request that you be evaluated by a mental health professional," the officer says.

"But we both know you can't take him into custody for that," I say.

The cops turn to stare at me, and I stare back, raising my eyebrows.

"Ma'am, we could certainly take him into custody if we see fit," the male officer drawls.

The way cops think they're smarter than everyone else, when they're bigger dipshits than three quarters of the population, makes me want to punch them all in their fucking throats. But I keep my composure. I smile. "Does he appear to be violent or mentally unstable to you? If his *mother* wishes him to be put away so that she can steal all his money, then she can speak to his lawyer, Patricia Harris at Harris, Castoro, and Miller. But it's not worth your jobs, I'm sure, to take a perfectly peaceful and law-abiding man into custody, and one who is certainly competent enough to pull off a very popular art opening in San Francisco."

That shuts them up. They know who Patty Harris is, sure as shit stinks. They shuffle their feet and exchange a doleful glance. The girl cop looks over at Justin. "You don't seem to be an imminent threat to yourself or others, Mr. Flaherty. We're just going to serve you with this paperwork, and leave it at that for now. Be sure to have your lawyer take a look at it right away, because you need to answer the petition within thirty days."

"I will," he murmurs.

The cops go out, and I stand there clenching and unclenching my fists, letting my rage drain out, letting my calm take over.

"What the fuck is going on here?" Liria says. She's still holding the kid's hand. She's in a cute little green and white dress, with bright blue hair, more beautiful than I've ever seen her.

"I just saved Justin's ass," I say, my voice husky despite my efforts. "Where's the gratitude?"

"Thank you very much, Arty," Justin says, and his voice makes me twitch. "But I'd also like to know what's going on, because it doesn't make sense that you would be taking an interest in these proceedings."

I glance over at Stewart. "You didn't tell me he was such a gentleman."

Stewart runs his hand through his hair and smiles sheepishly.

"Would you all please cut the crap?" Liria says, her brown eyes burning through me.

Stewart sighs, giving the kid a pathetic look. "I didn't want to, Justin," he says. "I would never have...but I think it will be better for you anyway…"

"What did you do, Stewart?" Liria moans.

I smile at her. "He did something that I think will turn out very well for all of us, *Christina.*" She flinches at the sound of her pseudonym, and I wince. I close my eyes and take a moment to let my hurt go away. I'm not here to fight with her anymore. I'm here to make her understand, to work this out.

The kid looks terrified, and I feel a wave of pity for him. He didn't ask for this, probably has no idea what's going on. He's just some mental doofus who likes to paint, the only person with any talent in this room, the worker bee surrounded by people craving honey. "Justin," I say, "I really apologize that we got off on the wrong foot. But I've been talking to Stewart, and I know now that I was wrong about you. You seem like a very nice and well-intentioned person, not to mention an extremely talented artist. Anyway, I'm sorry I was a jealous bitch. I hope we can start over, because I'd like to be friends."

"I'd like that too," he says, his brow furrowing. Liria has her lips screwed up, looking at me like I'm nuts. Well, maybe I am, but I can't help it. I love her, and I'll do fucking anything to get her back. Obviously.

"Anyway, I hope that we can have a good working relationship," I tell the kid.

He shoots Stewart a confused look. "I don't know what you mean."

Stewart grimaces. "Arty bought your contract. You're *her* new, amazing artist now."

The kid looks for a second like he's going to

faint, and Liria goes white. It hurts to see her upset about this, but I guess I don't blame her for misunderstanding. And we have all the time in the world to work this out now. I'll make her understand.

I smile at Justin. "We're going to make a lot of money, you and I."

Synchronicity

The Other Place Series

Book 4

Chapter 1

Liria and I lie on the hard, wooden floor of our new apartment, encapsulated like peanuts in our borrowed sleeping bags. I stare at the splashes of streetlight on the ceiling and listen to the man in the next apartment. He seems to be having an argument with his television, or maybe the television is having an argument with him.

Liria's sigh hisses through the empty corners of the room. "Arty is such a fucking asswipe."

I twist the slick fabric of my bag between my fingers. "Arty is a very cunning and deliberate person."

Liria rolls over, and her sleeping bag shoots little static sparks into the darkness. She regards me with her beautiful lips pulled into a frown, very close to mine. "I wonder what game she's playing."

"It's a game of the Dark Energy. You must see the patterns and parallels in this situation. They're lined up like wolves' teeth, along with Mom's petition and what Rebecca did. They're ready to bite us."

She puts her arm around me. She paints little tickling strokes on my neck, and her breath fills my lungs so that I'm dizzy with it. "I don't think those things have anything to do with one another," she says. "It's just a lot of shitty things happening all at once, that's all."

I gaze at her beautiful face. We're together in the Dark Energy, and I know Liria would never hurt me or trick me. But I don't know if she's right this time. She may be misreading the signs.

We lie in each other's arms. It's peaceful, but it also makes my heart ache and twists me up, because how I feel about her isn't how I should feel about her.

"Liria," I say, very carefully so as not to disturb the calmness, "Arty wants you back. She still loves you."

Liria is silent. My statement hangs in the air like a puff of vinegar-flavored smoke, slowly dissipating, dismembered by tendrils of Dark Energy.

"I don't think that's true," she finally says in a voice that's tiny like a bug. "I think she just wants your money."

"But my money is a thing that doesn't exist in the Physical World right now, actually, so her wanting it wouldn't be a strong enough force to compel her action because Other Place things don't have gravity like that, usually."

Liria sighs. "Justin…"

"I think it was a miscommunication between you two, and that you really love each other." My heart beats painfully. I twist and twist the sleeping bag until the zipper squeals in fear, and Liria gently pries my hands free.

She cradles both my hands in hers, tracing my fingers with her thumb. Her head is bowed and I can't see her face. "I...Arty's a jerk, Justin."

Her tickling thumbs make a bad environment for my agitation. My breath comes easier. "Everybody is a jerk sometimes, when the Dark Energy is telling them to do things that other people don't understand."

She looks up at me, her big eyes shining in the light that comes through the bare, warped windows. "I...I don't want to be with her anymore."

My fingers tap against hers. Her gaze encases me in beautiful glints. "Liria, I..." My words bunch up and form a lump in my throat, and I swallow them.

"Justin, what's wrong?"

I can't talk about the wrong feelings that are making garbage smells in the trash compactor of my stomach. "Liria, I need you in my life," I say instead. "I don't want to lose you."

"There's no way you're going to lose me." She hugs me tighter, all her curves pressed against me. "I need you too, Justin. I need you."

Slowly, I take deep breaths of her good smells. It's enough. It has to be enough.

Eventually, her warmth seeps into me, and I fall asleep.

***

We dream that night of sitting together on the banks of a clear creek fringed by willow trees. The wind whistles through the grass and hisses through the branches like fizzing soda bubbles. Fish with tiny, fleshy wheels attached to their bellies chase each other along the muddy banks, their lips wooing, their eyes emotionless. Crouching amongst the bendy top branches of the trees are a flock of vulture businessmen. They watch us silently, their unsettling stares piercing the Dark Energy.

Liria peers up at them through the rustling leaves, chewing on her lip. "Who are they, anyway?"

She says it very quietly and the businessmen jostle closer on the branches so they can hear.

"I don't know," I say. "But I don't think they have good intentions."

A shadow passes over us, making us jump and cling tight to one another. A creature of some sort is circling overhead, its large wings dark against the silver-blue sky.

***

A knock echoes through our empty apartment, jerking us back into the Physical World. Our eyes snap open, and we blink away the bleariness, our faces very close together. We're in each other's arms with our sleeping bags twisted around us, and the morning sun bursts through the big, uncovered windows.

The knock comes again. Each rap feels like the sting of a gigantic bee in my spine. I imagine an angry thug bee smacking the door with his brass knuckles, and I get the jitters. Then reality snuggles back too tight around me, and I realize it is probably not a huge, murderous bee, but something much, much worse. It is probably Arty, who said she was going to come over this morning.

Liria tosses her sleeping bag and pillow into a far corner of the room and tugs her fingers through her tangled blue hair. I pull on my jeans and go to the door, opening it quickly before I can change my mind.

Arty stands with her hands in the pockets of sleek, red slacks. Their color makes me taste pomegranate. There is a moment in which her expression is vulnerable and sad, then it freezes over and she gives me a smile I could shave with. "Good morning, Justin."

"Good morning, Ms. Kopanis. Please come in."

She wrinkles her nose. "Please, call me Arty. The only people who call me Ms. Kopanis are checkout clerks and the police."

"I'm not a checkout clerk or police." I step aside and she strides past me. Her eyes dart around the room, taking in the sleeping bags in opposite corners, and I'm glad Liria thought to separate them. Even though Liria and I are not together like that, I know Arty would think the wrong thing, and I'm pretty sure it would turn her into a demon who transmits the sickness.

"We should go get breakfast," Arty says. "We have a lot to discuss." Her eyes flick to Liria, who stands picking her cuticles with a face that tells me she smells all the bad smells in this situation. "You should come with us, Liria," Arty continues. "I know how you like free meals, and I'm paying."

Liria's fists clench at her sides. "Let me get dressed and brush my teeth." She stomps over and causes a commotion of flying clothing at her suitcase, stalks off into the bathroom, and shuts the door hard.

I'm alone with Arty, who examines me with a blank look. She's difficult for me to figure out. She must know about the Dark Energy, though, because I have never seen anyone that can control it the way she does.

"Arty," I say, "I don't understand what kind of test this is. If it's not against the rules, maybe you could just give me a hint."

Her green-blue eyes lose their blankness, like television screens turning on, but they're only showing static. "I guess I don't understand what kind of test this is either, Justin." She gives me a little smile. It's not a friendship or happiness smile, and I'm not sure what kind it is, but she must give it a lot because it activates the little wrinkles in her freckled cheeks.

I lick my dry lips. "I'm not sure I'm even supposed to pass it. Maybe the Dark Energy doesn't want me to reach enlightenment."

She frowns. "What was that, Justin? I didn't hear you."

I shift on my feet. "No, nothing. It was nothing."

Liria comes out of the bathroom and stops in her tracks, gazing back and forth between the two of us. She scowls at Arty. "What's going on?"

"Let's go," Arty says.

It is a beautiful day outside, the grungy San Francisco streets steaming in the golden sun. Liria walks beside me, squinting off at nothing with a pained look. I want to take her hand. I want to find some way to smooth the emotions out for her and make her feel better, but I don't know how, especially with Arty watching.

"I saw a little diner down here," Arty says, jerking her thumb down a side street. "You know if it's any good?"

Liria shrugs, shoving balled fists into the pockets of her kelly green shorts. "Never been there. We just moved in a few days ago, and don't have money for eating out."

"Let's give the place a shot," Arty says.

The restaurant has big windows and smells like fried ham. A waitress leads us to a booth with pinky-red vinyl seats, which must be what's giving off the smell. I'm uncomfortable with the prospect of sitting on a fat slab of pig, but I realize that Liria and Arty and the waitress are staring at me so I scrunch my guts up against the grossness and slide over the greasy surface.

Liria slides in next to me. Arty sits across from us, her eyes fixed on us like a wolf watching a pair of rabbits. I try not to twitch my ears and little nose and beguile her into a bloodlust pounce. I try not to think about the fact she is probably carrying a gun somewhere on her person, but that thought is there, sitting heavy on me, so if she does pounce I probably won't be able to hop away in time. I shift my butt on the squishy ham. I'm uncomfortable all around.

The waitress takes our orders for coffee, then waggles off into waitress land where the food happens. Arty smiles suddenly; I twitch, startled.

"Well," she says. "Your opening was a gigantic success, Justin. Every single last one of your pieces got offers, some of them multiple offers. You'll be buying *me* breakfast pretty soon."

Liria sits up straighter. "Really? That's awesome."

"I'm glad people like my pictures," I say.

"Well, it doesn't surprise me that they do," Arty says. "You're truly a genius, Justin. I mean, I'm not really an art person, and even I can see how good you are."

"When are you going to give Justin his money?" Liria asks. "And don't try to take more than your forty percent, Arty, because that's what the contract says."

Arty cocks an eyebrow at her. "Calm down, Liria. No one is going to try to steal *Justin's* money, or at least *I* don't plan on it." She gives Liria her sharp little smile, and Liria crosses her arms and glares. Arty rolls her eyes back to mine. "But we're not going to sell most of the pieces right now."

"What do you mean?" Liria says. "If people want to buy them, then let them. Justin needs money. I mean I…I'm barely making enough to cover rent." Liria picks at her cuticles and stares at her lap. The green, embarrassing haze of our money situation settles on us like fart smell.

Arty blinks. Her wolfish slyness seems to have been startled off. "You're working?"

Liria huffs out her nose. The waitress comes up with our coffees and smiles around at us, asks if we're ready to order.

We remember we're in a restaurant, and that our purpose in being here is supposedly to eat food. Arty and Liria stammer out vague requests including bacon and sides of fruit. I try to picture the type of food that belongs in my stomach in this situation, and can't. I ask for oatmeal in the hopes it's slimy enough to slide in between my other stomach slime.

The waitress's cheerful presence withdraws, leaving us to bask in squirminess. "*Yes,*" Liria resumes. "I'm working."

"Where at?" Arty asks.

"A coffee shop."

Arty studies her for a few more moments, then looks back at me, frowning slightly as she tries to rearrange the shreds of her wolf costume into order. "If we sold all the pieces now, you wouldn't have anything left for other shows. And we can get even more money if we hold out. Your popularity is already growing, and if I know anything about business, increase in demand means increase in price."

"He'll paint some more pictures by the time he has another show," Liria says. "He gets them done really fast, a couple a week sometimes."

"So he wouldn't have many. I've set him up another show in New York in two weeks."

This statement drops onto our heads like a piano. Liria and I look wide-eyed at each other.

"New York?" Liria says quietly. "But, Arty…"

"I've got it all worked out," Arty cuts in, giving her a dark look. "We'll have to leave in a week to get ready."

Liria shifts in her seat, the pig-vinyl squealing. "When you say 'we'…"

"I mean you too. You're an important part of this team."

Liria gapes. "But New *York,* Arty?"

"You're coming," Arty says.

Liria leans forward, gripping the table, her eyes darting around the restaurant. "You spent six months telling me not to leave the house so that I wouldn't be in danger of being recognized. And now you want to go to New *York*? The place Peter Czetski *lives*? You're supposed to be *dead*, Arty, and I vouched that you were—"

"I told you," Arty says, quiet and slow, "I've got it all worked out."

I think to myself that this is pretty exciting, actually. I've never met anyone who was supposed to be dead before.

Liria stomps and speaks quietly, though her angry words make explosions in the Dark Energy that are very visible. "Was it just bullshit all along, about needing to stay hidden? Were you just trying to control me?"

The waitress comes up with the coffee pot, regards the uncomfortable situation and the fact none of us have remembered to drink our coffee, and scurries off again like she's seeking shelter from a ticking bomb.

"It wasn't bullshit," Arty says. "But I have a plan."

They stare at one another. My heart pounds. I can hear the soundtrack to an action thriller movie playing in the Dark Energy.

Liria's eyes drop out of the staring contest. "I can't go anyway. I've got work. They'll never let me have more than couple days off."

"Quit your stupid job, then."

"Arty, I can't quit my job. We need the money."

"You're fucking going, Christina. I need you to keep...things...from going all crazy." She smiles sweetly at me before looking back at Liria, and I curl around my coffee cup, because I may be what she calls a crazy thing, but I'm not mentally challenged enough to not know I'm the crazy thing to which she refers.

"Besides," Arty continues, "you don't need your job. I'm sure Justin won't mind paying rent for a while. After all, when all the deals are closed from last night, his take is going to be over thirty grand."

Liria blinks at me. I pour some cream into my coffee and stir it, watching it swirl. The notion of all that money buzzes around me like a fly, but I don't quite notice it.

"*Thirty thousand*?" Liria says.

"Yes, roughly," Arty says.

I look up from my coffee. Arty is watching Liria closely.

"A couple of them are still in bidding wars, so it may go higher," she says. "I'll let you see an accounting once it's all done."

I blink as that buzzing money-fly finally lands on my nose. I shake my head to dislodge it, but it returns. "Excuse me, did you just say I have thirty thousand dollars?"

"That's what she said," Liria says.

I look back at my coffee, squeezing the smooth

porcelain cup tight in my hand. "I'm going to lose my social security money, like Mom said." The thoughts of Mom and money and all these things happening right now start up a trailer trash fight in my head, which is very hard to look away from. Mom throws a coffee cup at me and I half-duck before I realize I don't have to do that in the Physical World.

"It's going to be okay, Justin," Liria says. "You're going to make enough money that you won't need your social security."

Arty slurps her coffee and sets the mug down with a thump. "Let your attorney worry about the social security money. Speaking of which, we need to discuss the petition your fuckhead of a mother filed."

I twitch as something touches my thigh. I look over and see it's Liria's hand, and that she's gazing at me with big, worried eyes. My shoulders are hunched and my face is scrunched up, like someone has tightened my spiritual drawstring. I sit up straighter, rolling my shoulders and imagining the mind-police hauling my trailer trash thoughts off to the drunk tank. I take a deep breath and blow it out. "Mom is part of the trap, I think. Does the attorney you hired know about those sorts of traps?"

Arty gazes at me. Liria squeezes my thigh. The waitress brings our food, but no one seems to notice except Arty, who picks up her fork and spears a grape from her bowl of fruit.

"I spoke to Patty Harris this morning," Arty says, crunching the grape like a wolf gnawing a rabbit's head. "She's the lawyer, and she's really good. She says your mom doesn't have much of a chance of success, as long as we play our cards right. Stewart and I will write declarations that you've entered into fair and legitimate business contracts with us and are running your affairs satisfactorily. Liria will say that you're her roommate, that you pay your share of rent and expenses, toss your dirty socks in the laundry basket, and always put the toilet seat down. All you have to do is keep it together in public." She raises her eyebrows at me. "And I mean, no breakdowns or any of that fainty bullshit you pulled when I showed up at my apartment. Actually, I'd appreciate it if you just kept your mouth shut as much as possible when we're around people. Can you do that?"

Liria huffs. "Arty…"

Arty's eyes don't leave my face. "Let him answer."

Liria crosses her arms and looks away. I look back at my coffee.

"Well?" Arty says.

"I don't know what this test is," I say to my coffee. "I don't know how to pass it, so I don't think I should say anything right now."

Arty sighs heavily. I imagine that it's my coffee sighing at me, because I don't want to look at Arty or remember about her at all.

"You're upsetting him!" Liria whisper-shouts, her fingers clenching my thigh.

"I'm just trying to do what's best for him and his career," Arty says.

Liria snorts. "Good one. You're doing what's best for you."

I hear Arty take a breath to add to the growing pile of angry words when I speak up. "Please don't argue. It's not appropriate for the restaurant atmosphere, or any atmosphere. I'm certain it's contributing to climate change at this point, actually."

Both of them go silent. I glance up to see Arty regarding me with the corners of her mouth twitching up. She and Liria both giggle. It's the first time I've seen them laugh together, and I suddenly remember they used to be girlfriends. It makes me feel like my heart is collapsing on itself.

Liria sighs. Under the table, her hand unclenches from my thigh, and her fingers creep over to interlock with mine. "I'm sorry, Justin." Her giggle is completely gone, and her big eyes squint up with tears. "I didn't mean to upset you."

I like the feeling of her hand in mine, though I worry Arty can somehow see through the table and know it's happening. I stroke Liria's thumb with mine. "Don't cry, Liria."

Liria wipes her eyes. Arty massages the skin between her eyebrows for a moment before she picks up her knife and smears cream cheese on her bagel with violent strokes. "I'm sorry too, Justin. I don't want to argue. Just, you know, try to keep it together. *Please*. If you feel like you're going to faint or…whatever…tell one of us, okay?"

Liria looks at me. Under the table, she puts her foot next to mine.

"I will try to do that, Arty," I say, because I'm not sure what else to say.

"Thank you, Justin." Arty munches her bagel,

and Liria drops my hand, picks up a slice of bacon and stirs it around in her pancake syrup as if it's the saddest thing she's ever done. I remember about my oatmeal, and try to organize my mind around the idea of eating.

"By the way, Justin," Arty says. "Since all that bullshit happened at the opening and you weren't able to go out with Mina last night, I talked to her. She's still in town today. She's going to meet you for a little date at three o'clock."

Liria stops with her bacon halfway to her mouth, dripping syrup onto her plate. "*What,* Arty? *No.*"

"What's your problem?" Arty says. "She's his girlfriend."

"Not anymore," Liria says. "That bitch dumped him, and now she wants to torture him by trying to get back together."

I wad myself up like a used tissue around my slimy snot feelings.

Arty gazes at Liria and stabs her poor fruit. "Fine. I'll call Mina and tell her you can't see her today."

"No, I think I should see her."

Liria huffs. "Justin…"

"I think the social dance says I have to see her, because there are wild emotions running around, and if we don't round them up they may trample us all to death."

Liria snickers, and look over to see her smiling. She is so beautiful. "You're right," she says. "But I just don't want her to hurt you."

"She can't hurt me any more than she already has. Those emotions are already galloping free."

Liria presses her lips together, and she nods. "Okay. But just…just call me, if she upsets you, and I'll come get you, okay?"

"Okay, Liria."

Arty taps her fingers against her forearms, watching us from inside a cloud of churning, unreadable thoughts.

Acknowledgments

I wrote this series during one of the darkest periods in my life, and in my life, that's saying something. There were a lot of people that brought light into it, though, and I'd like to thank them. Without them, this series wouldn't be published, and I'd be either dead or quickly on my way there.

My daughter, Juniper, who always told me when I was crossing that line into dangerous and self-destructive territory, but also would tell me when I was doing the right thing. I look at how happy and vibrant you are now, and I know that I've been a good enough person despite it all, because a horrible mother wouldn't have such a smart and well-adjusted kid.

My parents, my friends Mari, Aleena, Faith, Gary, Naomi, Tracy, Devon, who were all there to treat me with kindness and remind me I could climb out of my hellish situation if I wanted. Devon, I know we're split on political and religious issues right now, but I still love you.

My critique groups, who are also friends: Mike, Jeannie, Katie, Chaitanya, Lillian, Joey, Aaron. You were my life raft.

And, of course, Phoenix. You never caused a problem you couldn't solve for me. You, to me, are nothing more than an example of the fact that the darkness of the Physical World means nothing, because its heart and source are always beauty. You showed me a life more meaningful than existence. I'm sorry I left. I had to put the world askew in order to straighten my life. The Physical World works that way sometimes, and it tears at our cores. It's up to you, now, to put it right. I'll wait, and I'll always come back.

About the Author

Elizabeth Roderick grew up as a barefoot ruffian on a fruit orchard near Yakima, in the eastern part of Washington State. After weathering the grunge revolution and devolution in Olympia, Washington, Portland, Oregon and Seattle, she recently moved to the (very, very) small town of Shandon, California: a small cluster of houses amidst the vineyards of the Central Coast.

She earned a bachelor's degree in Spanish from The Evergreen State College in Olympia, Washington, and worked for many years as a paralegal and translator. She went on to study chemistry, physics, and higher mathematics, with the goal of becoming a research chemist, but was eventually forced to concede that graduate school would require too much time away from her husband and daughter, and that–despite her good-enough grades–she was perhaps the wrong kind of nerd for such pursuits, being more the type that likes to dress in cloaks and hauberks rather than lab coats and goggles.

She is a musician and songwriter, and has played in many bands. She's rocked pretty much every instrument, including some she doesn't even know the real names for, but mostly guitar, bass and keyboards. She has two albums of her own, which you can listen to at pimentointhehole.com. She writes fiction novels for young adults and adults, as well as short stories, and keeps an active blog at pimentointhehole.com/blog.

Facebook:
https://www.facebook.com/elizabethroderickauthor

Twitter:
https://twitter.com/LidsRodney

Website:
http://talesfrompurgatory.com/